Ian Rankin

The Falls

An Orion paperback

First published in Great Britain in 2001
by Orion
This paperback edition published in 2001
by Orion Books Ltd,
Orion House, 5 Upper St Martin's Lane,
London WC2H 9EA

An Hachette Livre UK company

Reissued 2008

A CIP catalogue record for this book is available from the British Library.

Printed and bound in Great Britain by Clays Ltd, St Ives plc

The Orion Publishing Group's policy is to use papers that are natural, renewable and recyclable products and made from wood grown in sustainable forests. The logging and manufacturing processes are expected to conform to the environmental regulations of the country of origin.

www.orionbooks.co.uk

Praise for Ian Rankin

'Rankin's ability to create a credible character, delivering convincing dialogue to complement sinister and hard-hitting plots set against vividly detailed atmosphere, is simply awesome' *Time Out*

'Rankin is streets ahead in the British police procedural writing field . . . our top crime writer'
Independent on Sunday

'His ear for dialogue is as sharp as a switchblade. This is, quite simply, crime writing of the highest order' *Daily Express*

'Rankin writes laconic, sophisticated, well-paced thrillers' *Scotsman*

'Ian Rankin bridges the gulf between the straight novel and the mystery with enviable ease'
Allan Massie

'First-rate crime fiction with a fierce realism'
Sunday Telegraph

'Rankin uses his laconic prose as a literary paint stripper, scouring away pretensions to reveal the unwholesome reality beneath' *Independent*

'His fiction buzzes with energy . . . Essentially, he is a romantic storyteller in the tradition of Robert Louis Stevenson . . . His prose is as vivid and terse as the next man's, yet its flexibility and rhythm give it a potential for lyrical expression which is distinctively Rankin's own' *Scotland on Sunday*

By Ian Rankin

The Inspector Rebus series
Knots & Crosses
Hide & Seek
Tooth & Nail
Strip Jack
The Black Book
Mortal Causes
Let It Bleed
Black & Blue
The Hanging Garden
Death Is Not the End (*novella*)
Dead Souls
Set in Darkness
The Falls
Resurrection Men
A Question of Blood
Fleshmarket Close
The Naming of the Dead
Exit Music

Other novels
The Flood
Watchman
Westwind

Writing as Jack Harvey
Witch Hunt
Bleeding Hearts
Blood Hunt

Short stories
A Good Hanging and Other Stories
Beggars Banquet

Omnibus editions
Rebus: The Early Years (Knots & Crosses, Hide & Seek, Tooth & Nail)
Rebus: The St Leonard's Years (Strip Jack, The Black Book, Mortal Causes)
Rebus: The Lost Years (Let It Bleed, Black & Blue, The Hanging Garden)
Rebus: Capital Crimes (Dead Souls, Set in Darkness, The Falls)

Non-fiction
Rebus's Scotland

All Ian Rankin's titles are available on audio.
Also available: *Jackie Leven Said* by Ian Rankin and Jackie Leven.

Born in the Kingdom of Fife in 1960, Ian Rankin graduated from the University of Edinburgh in 1982, and then spent three years writing novels when he was supposed to be working towards a PhD in Scottish Literature. His first Rebus novel, *Knots & Crosses*, was published in 1987, and the Rebus books are now translated into over thirty languages and are bestsellers worldwide.

Ian Rankin has been elected a Hawthornden Fellow, and is also a past winner of the Chandler-Fulbright Award. He is the recipient of four Crime Writers' Association Dagger Awards including the prestigious Diamond Dagger in 2005. In 2004, Ian won America's celebrated Edgar award for *Resurrection Men*. He has also been shortlisted for the Anthony Awards in the USA, and won Denmark's *Palle Rosenkrantz* Prize, the French *Grand Prix du Roman Noir* and the *Deutscher Krimipreis*. Ian Rankin is also the recipient of honorary degrees from the universities of Abertay, St Andrews, Edinburgh, Hull and the Open University.

A contributor to BBC2's *Newsnight Review*, he also presented his own TV series, *Ian Rankin's Evil Thoughts*. He has received the OBE for services to literature, opting to receive the prize in his home city of Edinburgh. He has also recently been appointed to the rank of Deputy Lieutenant of Edinburgh, where he lives with his partner and two sons. Visit his website at www.ianrankin.net.